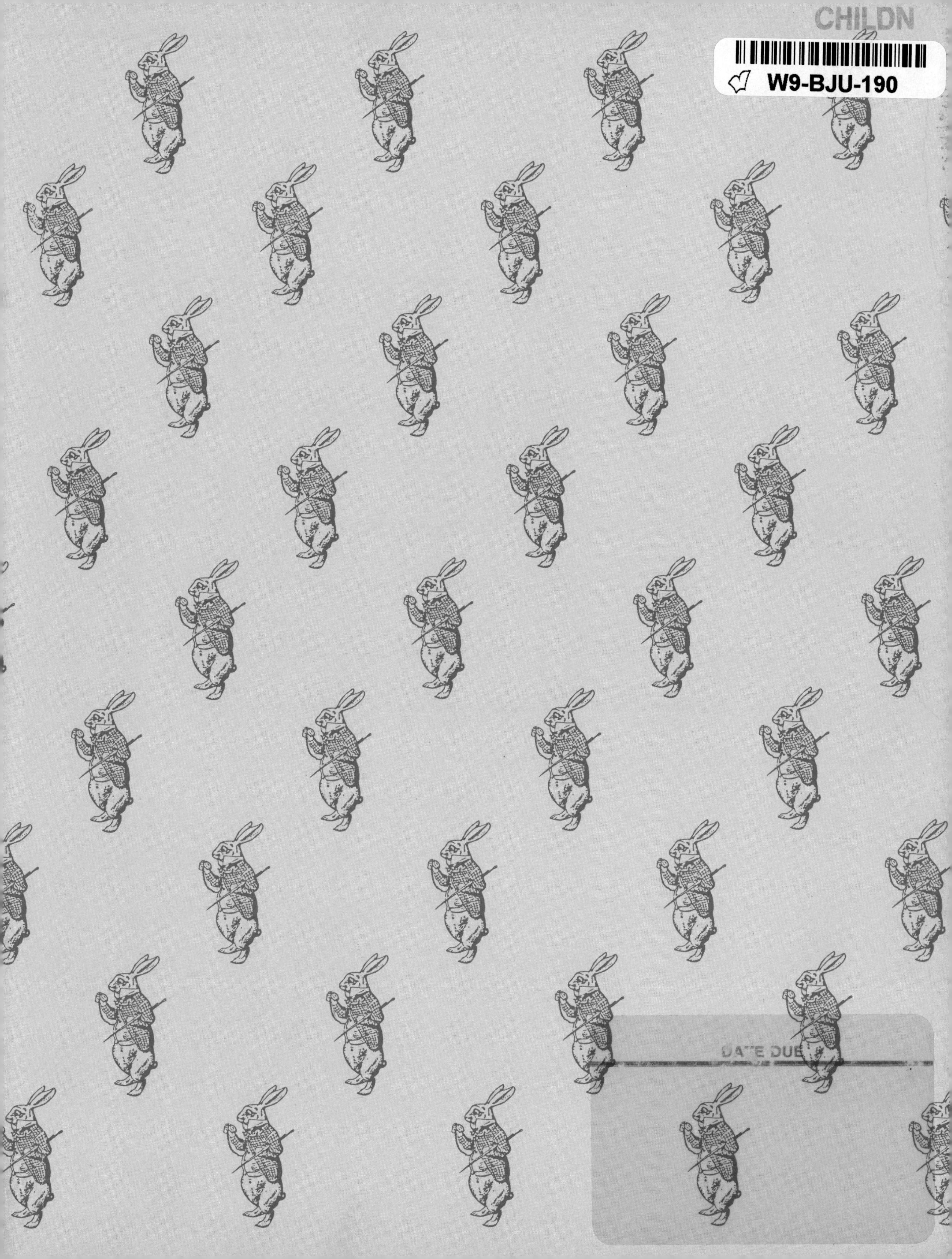
CHILDN
W9-BJU-190
DATE DUE

Typeset in the United States of America: Printed in Hong Kong

Published by Alyson Wonderland,
an imprint of Alyson Publications, Inc.,
P.O. Box 4371, Los Angeles, California 90078.

First edition: June 1996

5 4 3 2 1

ISBN 1-55583-350-0

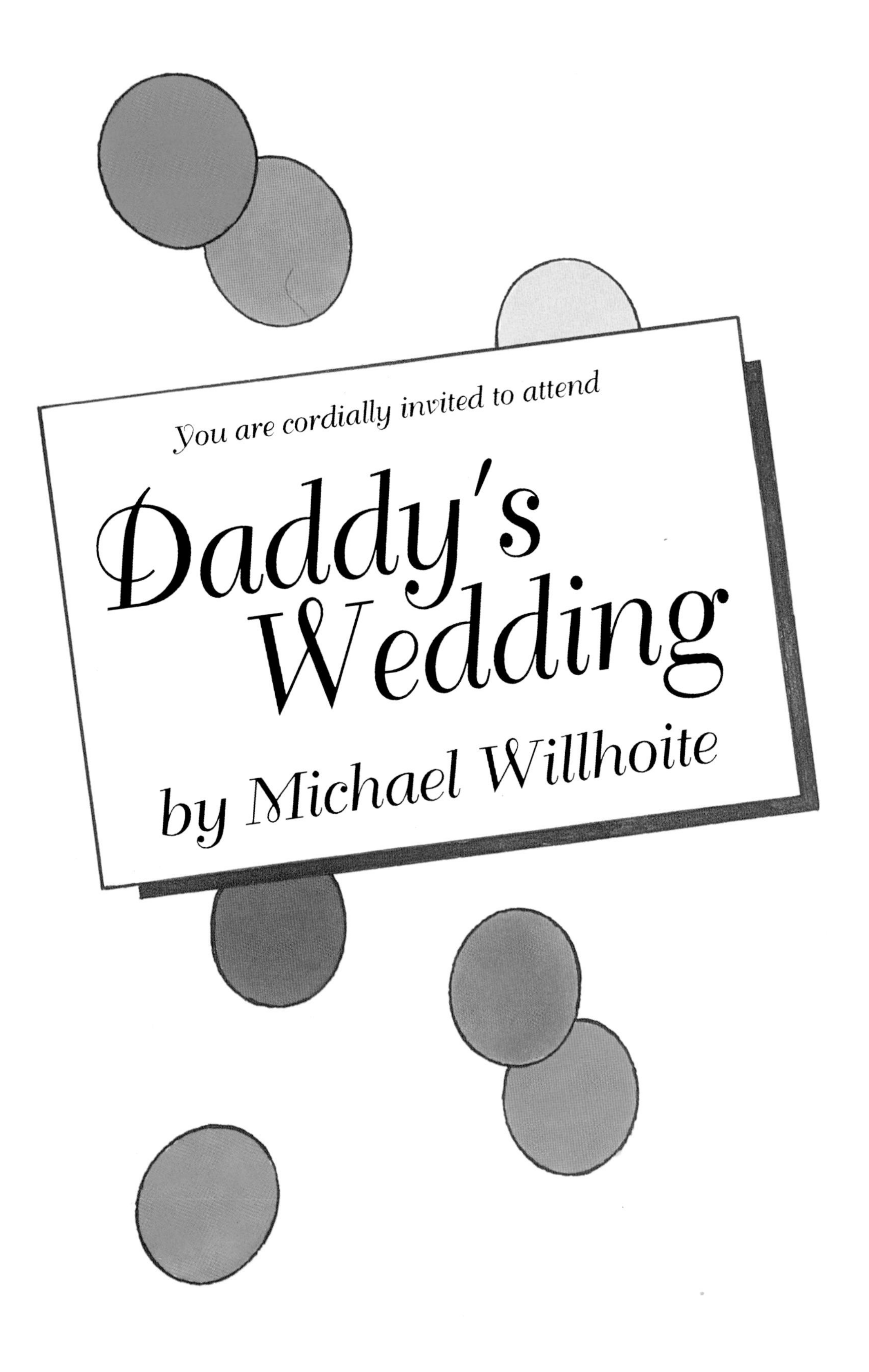
You are cordially invited to attend
Daddy's Wedding
by Michael Willhoite

Dedication:

To Nellie and Johnny Perry,
loving partners in a wonderful marriage.

One day Mommy and Steven and I had a picnic in our back yard. Steven is my new stepfather. He can play the guitar and loves baseball as much as I do!

“Hey, Nick,” Steven said, “Why don’t you go play. I’ll barbecue the chicken.”

My friends wanted to play volleyball. Soon we were thirsty, so Mommy served us her special strawberry punch.

Daddy and his roommate Frank were the last to arrive. Clancy came, too.

Clancy's a great dog, but he sure can get in the way!

When the picnic was almost over, Daddy and Frank took me to the garden swing to talk. Daddy said, "Nick, we want to invite you to a special occasion next month. We're going to get married."

"Can men get married to each other?" I asked.

"We call it a commitment ceremony, Nick," said Frank. "That's like a wedding." Mommy and Steven joined us, and Daddy and Frank told them about it. "We want you all to come," Daddy said.

Mommy hugged Daddy and said, “We’d love to, Daniel! It sounds like a lot of fun. Nothing’s better than a wedding in June.”

Daddy turned and said, “Nick, would you do me the honor of being my best man? We want you to be an important part of our big day.” And Frank said, “You’re the first one we thought of.”

This was terrific! "I'd love to, Dad," I said. "I'll be the *best* best man you've ever seen!"

On the day of the wedding, we drove to Daddy and Frank's house on the other side of town.

The yard was filled with people. There were flowers everywhere. Balloons and flags hung from the trees.

My Grandma and Grandpa were already there. A lot of Daddy and Frank's friends came, too.

Mommy and Steven sat together in the front row. I stood beside Reverend Powell, waiting for Daddy and Frank to come out of the house.

Music started playing, and Daddy and Frank appeared, looking *very* happy. When the music ended, Reverend Powell said, "Daniel and Frank have written vows they'd like to read."

First, Daddy told us how he met Frank. Then Daddy turned to Frank and said, "I'm looking forward to spending the rest of my life with you."

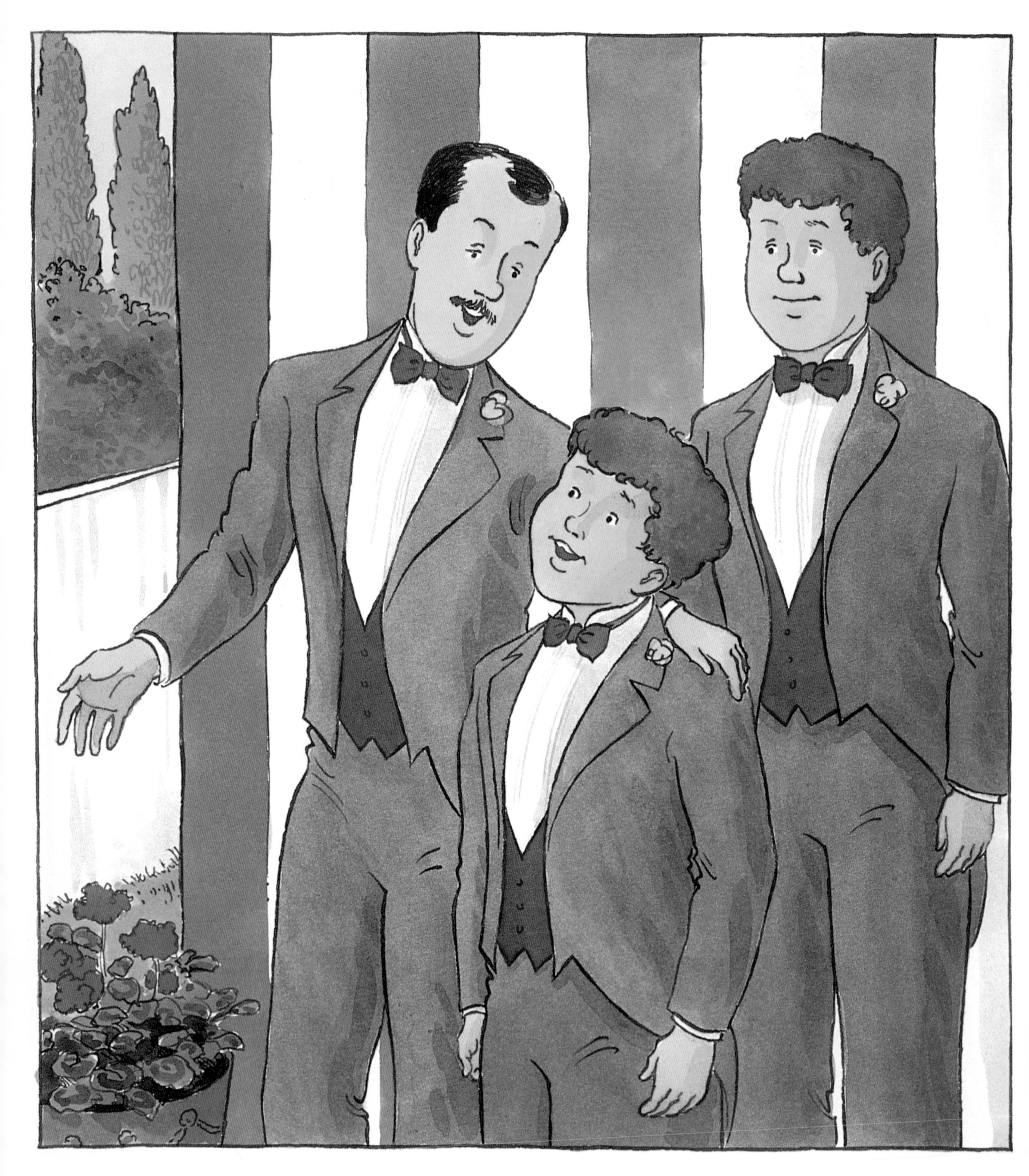

Then Frank spoke. He vowed to love Daddy, and take care of him in sickness and in health. Frank turned to me. "And we already have a son to share." That was my favorite part of the wedding.

Reverend Powell turned to me. "Nick, I believe you have the rings."

First, Daddy put a gold ring on Frank's finger. Then Frank slipped a ring on Daddy's finger.

After that, Reverend Powell said they were married. And suddenly hundreds of balloons fell down all over the place!

Reverend Powell said, “Daniel and Frank’s friends have prepared a lovely reception. Let’s enjoy ourselves!”

Everyone turned to the tables at the side of the yard, where there were plates of sandwiches, bowls of punch, and a huge white wedding cake...

And Clancy!

"You *bad* dog!" Grandma said. "Ruining that lovely cake..." But Daddy and Frank just laughed.

“It’s just a little messed up, and only on this side,” I said. “And look, it still tastes good!”

The cake really *was* good. We all drank punch and ate until we almost busted — although Clancy managed to get into the sandwiches, too.

The day after the wedding, Daddy and Frank went to San Francisco for their honeymoon. I hope they had as much fun as I did that week...

I went to baseball camp!

OUR
Wedding

ALYSON
WONDERLAND